This book belongs to:

~~Dave~~

....

First published in 2016 by Hodder & Stoughton

Hodder Children's Books
An imprint of Hachette Children's Group, part of Hodder & Stoughton
Carmelite House, 50 Victoria Embankment, London, EC4Y 0DZ

Text copyright © Sue Hendra 2016. Illustrations copyright © Lee Wildish 2016

A catalogue record of this book is available from the British Library.

ISBN 978 1 444 92556 2

Printed in China

An Hachette UK Company.
www.hachette.co.uk

DOUBLE DAVE

Written by
Sue Hendra

Illustrated by
Lee Wildish

𝒽
Hodder
Children's
Books

Dave was big and quite fantastic, and so were his dinners. They were the envy of everyone in the garden.

Dave woke up hungry.
He popped through his cat flap
but where was his dinner?

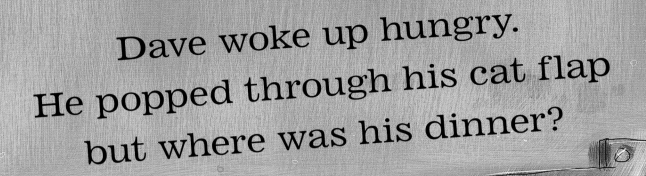

'You just ate it, Dave,'
said Bug.

I DID? thought Dave.
I don't remember doing that.

I don't remember doing that either.

I'm sure I didn't do that.

And I definitely didn't do that!

But if Dave didn't,
then WHO did?

Someone was sleeping in Dave's bed!

It was orange just like Dave.
It was big just like Dave.

But it couldn't be Dave!

thought Dave.

The new
Dave liked
Dave's
dinners.

The new Dave
liked Dave's bed.

The new Dave liked Dave's friends.

What could Dave do?

Luckily Bug had a plan.
'You can't both be the
real Dave,' said Bug.
'There's only one way
to find out for sure.'

So Bug made two *special* dinners.
'May the best Dave win!

READY, STEADY, GO!'

They
CHOMPED...

They
GUZZLED...

They
SLURPED...

until...

We have a winner!

Dave couldn't believe it.
I thought *I* was the real Dave!
thought Dave.

But as Dave watched,
the winner began to shake.
His tummy was RUMBLING.

Suddenly one of his ears flew off.

Then his head swizzled round.

Something BIG was about to happen...

5 4 3 2 1...

'Squirrels?!' said Bug.
'I might have known! They
are always up to mischief!'

Well, I suppose I *am* the real
Dave after all, thought Dave. Phew!
And he knew just how to celebrate...

...with a double dinner and a nap!